Through the Gate

D0902984

For anyone who has ever struggled with change.

For my family and especially my children, who
I hope will carry the message of this story with
them through the inevitable challenges and changes
of life as they learn and grow.

– S.F.

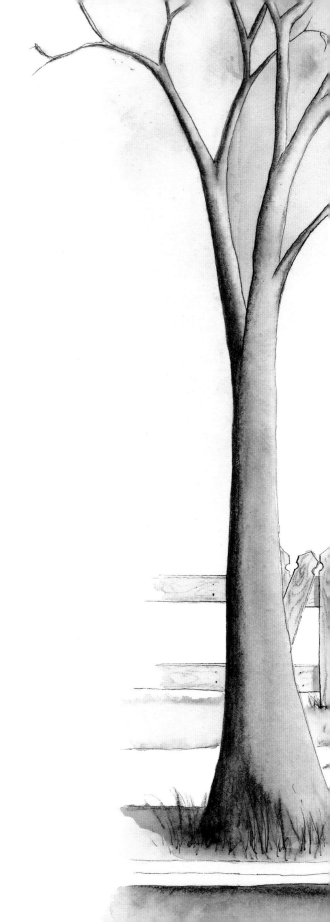

First published 2017
This edition published 2019

EK Books
an imprint of Exisle Publishing Pty Ltd
P.O. Box 864, Chatswood, NSW 2057, Australia
226 High Street, Dunedin 9016, New Zealand
www.ekbooks.org

A CiP record for this book is available from the National Library
of Australia.

ISBN 978-1-925820-09-6

Designed by Big Cat Design
Typeset in Sabon Roman 18 on 24pt
Printed in China

This book uses paper sourced under ISO 14001 guidelines from
well-managed forests and other controlled sources.

10 9 8 7 6 5 4 3 2 1

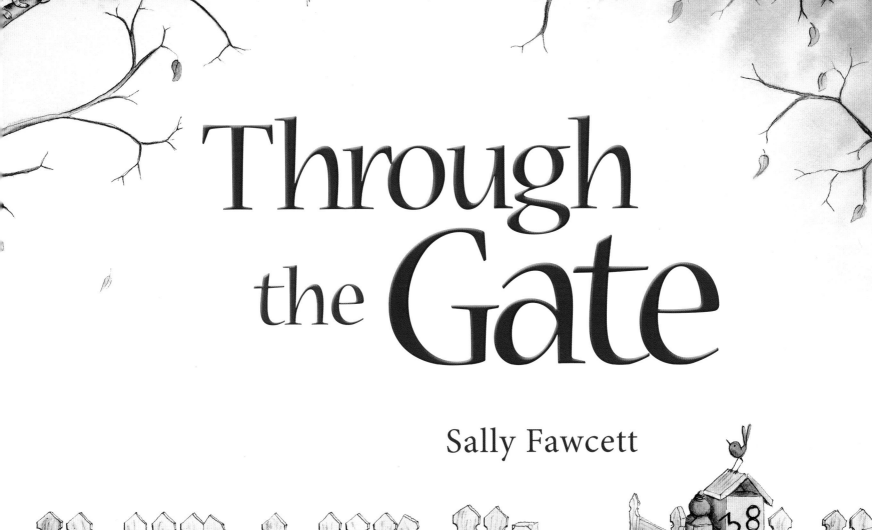

Through the Gate

Sally Fawcett

I first saw our 'new' house from the front gate.
It certainly wasn't new.

The roof was drooping.
The paint was peeling.
The step was crumbling.

Everywhere I looked I saw cracks.

I sat on the broken front step of the 'new' house.

New town, new school ... nothing was the same.

I plodded to school ... I plodded home ...

I plodded all week long.

I glared at my shoes and noticed the laces.

My laces had come undone.

On Friday I stopped at our gate.

I glared at the old house ahead.

Something was different.

I mooched to school … I mooched home …

I mooched all week long.

I stared at the ground and noticed some flowers. I picked a few for my mother.

On Friday I stopped at our gate.

I stared at the old house ahead.

Something was different.

I wandered to school … I wandered home …

I wandered all week long.

I gazed ahead and noticed a puppy.

I patted him on his tummy.

On Friday I stopped at our gate.

I gazed at the old house ahead.

Something was different.

I walked to school …

I walked home …

I walked all week long.

I looked around and noticed a girl.

I invited her to join me.

On Friday I stopped at our gate.

I looked at the old house ahead.

Something was different.

I marched to school …

I marched home …

I marched all week long.

I saw a bird then noticed a tree.

I tasted the sweetest plum.

On Friday I stopped at our gate.

I saw our house ahead.

Something was definitely different.

The old house looked new.

How did that happen while I was at school?

Then I felt something else change.

I had a new smile!

I skipped through the gate and into …

... our home.